Ff Gg Hh Ii

Nn Oo Pp Qq

Vv Ww Xx Yy

Zz

First published in 1990 by Usborne Publishing Ltd
Usborne House, 83-85 Saffron Hill, London EC1N 8RT.

Printed in Great Britain

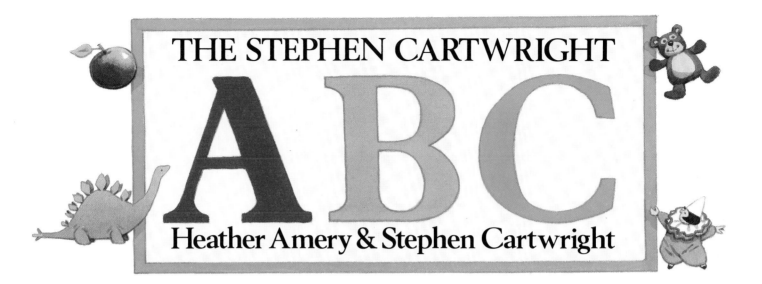

THE STEPHEN CARTWRIGHT
ABC

Heather Amery & Stephen Cartwright

Aa

A is for Alex, Andrew and Anne
Who gave an apple to their old gran.

B is for Betty, Billy and Bret
Who bought a butterfly as a pet.

Cc

C is for Corinne, Chris and Carol
Who caught a crocodile in a barrel.

Dd

D is for Daisy, Daniel and Dave
Who dragged a dinosaur from its cave.

Ee

E is for Emily, Ed and Elaine
Who washed an elephant in the rain.

Ff

F is for Fanny, Felix and Fred
Who hid from fireworks under the bed.

Gg

G is for Gordon, Gertie and Greg
Who gave a gorilla a golden egg.

Hh

H is for Helen, Henry and Hank
Whose house is on a green river bank.

Ii

I is for Ingrid, Ike and Irene
Who painted an igloo pink and green.

Jj

J is for Julie, Jenny and John
Who made a jelly to jump about on.

K k

K is for Katie, Kaspar and Koo
Who ran away with a kangaroo.

Ll

L is for Leo, Lucy and Lynn
Who tickled a lion under its chin.

Mm

M is for Martin, Maggie and Mark
Who sat with a monster in the dark.

N is for Nancy, Nicky and Ned
Who found a nest all made out of bread.

O is for Olive, Oscar, Odette
Who caught an ostrich in a net.

Pp

P is for Peter, Polly and Pat
Who played with a pig in a big pink hat.

Qq

Q is for Quentin, Quincy and Quin
Who had tea with a queen, tall and thin.

Rr

R is for Robert, Richard and Rose
Who danced up a rainbow on their toes.

Ss

S is for Simon, Sadie and Sue
Who sailed in a sandal when the wind blew.

T is for Tina, Thomas and Ted
Who taught a tiger to stand on its head.

Uu

U is for Ulwin and Ursula too
Who bought an umbrella and away they flew.

Vv

V is for Vera, Vivian and Vance
Who saw a volcano and ripped their pants.

Ww

W is for Wendy, Wanda and Will
Who worked a windmill on top of a hill.

X is for Xerxes and Xanthe , it's true
Who played a xylophone, shiny and new.

Yy

Y is for Yolanda and Yvette
Who ate fruit yogurt, cool and wet.

Zz

Z is for Zoe, Zara and Zack
Who went to the zoo and never came back.

A a

B b C c D d E e

J j K k L l M m

R r S s T t U u